MANDIE®
AND THE GRADUATION MYSTERY

Mandie® Mysteries

1. *Mandie and the Secret Tunnel*
2. *Mandie and the Cherokee Legend*
3. *Mandie and the Ghost Bandits*
4. *Mandie and the Forbidden Attic*
5. *Mandie and the Trunk's Secret*
6. *Mandie and the Medicine Man*
7. *Mandie and the Charleston Phantom*
8. *Mandie and the Abandoned Mine*
9. *Mandie and the Hidden Treasure*
10. *Mandie and the Mysterious Bells*
11. *Mandie and the Holiday Surprise*
12. *Mandie and the Washington Nightmare*
13. *Mandie and the Midnight Journey*
14. *Mandie and the Shipboard Mystery*
15. *Mandie and the Foreign Spies*
16. *Mandie and the Silent Catacombs*
17. *Mandie and the Singing Chalet*
18. *Mandie and the Jumping Juniper*
19. *Mandie and the Mysterious Fisherman*
20. *Mandie and the Windmill's Message*
21. *Mandie and the Fiery Rescue*
22. *Mandie and the Angel's Secret*
23. *Mandie and the Dangerous Imposters*
24. *Mandie and the Invisible Troublemaker*
25. *Mandie and Her Missing Kin*
26. *Mandie and the Schoolhouse's Secret*
27. *Mandie and the Courtroom Battle*
28. *Mandie and Jonathan's Predicament*
29. *Mandie and the Unwanted Gift*
30. *Mandie and the Long Good-bye*
31. *Mandie and the Buried Stranger*
32. *Mandie and the Seaside Rendezvous*
33. *Mandie and the Dark Alley*
34. *Mandie and the Tornado!*
35. *Mandie and the Quilt Mystery*
36. *Mandie and the New York Secret*
37. *Mandie and the Night Thief*
38. *Mandie and the Hidden Past*
39. *Mandie and the Missing Schoolmarm*
40. *Mandie and the Graduation Mystery*

Mandie and Mollie: The Angel's Visit

04C